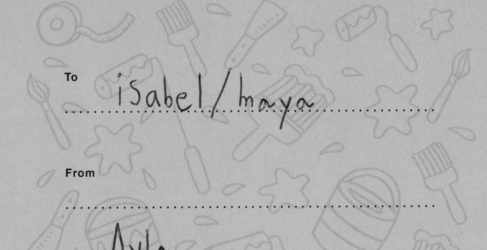

To ......isabel/maya...

From ....

......Ayla..

Author Bob Wise is the founder of one of the world's largest music publishing organisations. *This Isn't My House* is his second children's book to feature the well-meaning but accident-prone brother mice *Hickory Dickory & Doc*.

IMAGINE & WONDER™ Publishers, New York

BishBash BOOKS

New York & London

This Isn't My House

Hickory Dickory&Doc

a story by Bob Wise, illustrated by Sonia Canals

Hickory, **Dickory** and **Doc** were
three brothers who had been successfully
running a clock making business.

Now they felt it was time
to start another business
they could run together.

They decided on house painting.

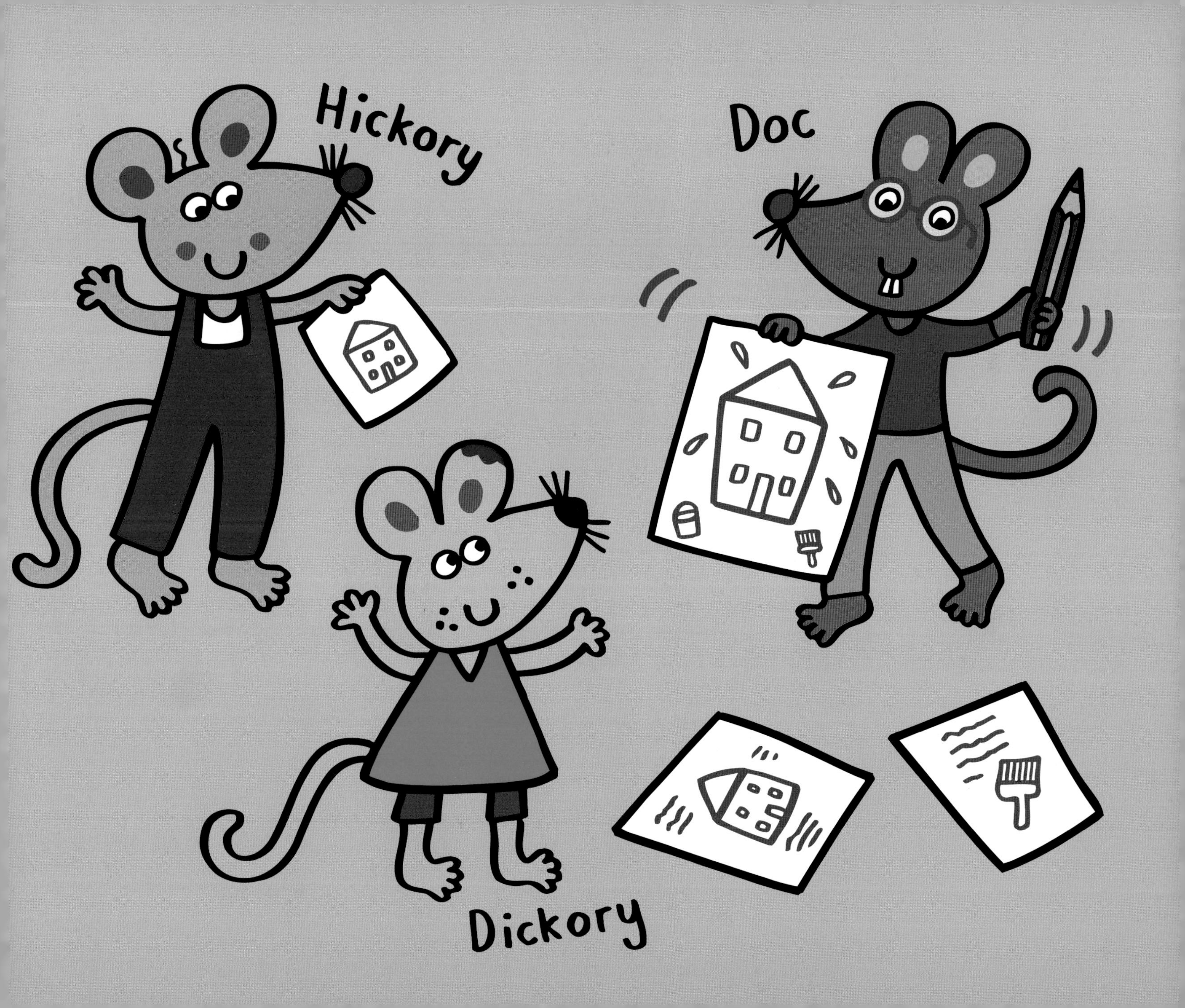
Hickory
Doc
Dickory

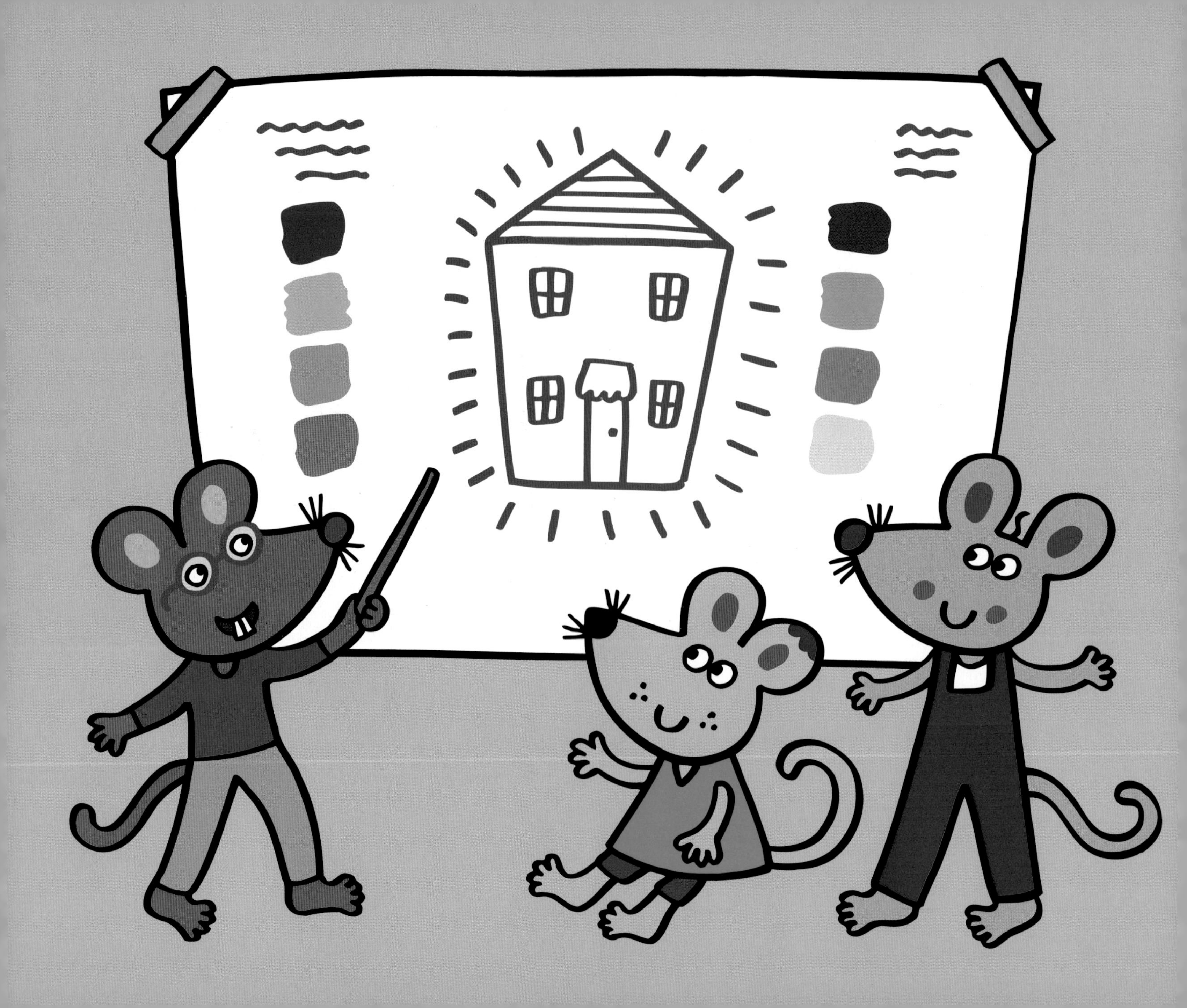

To make their business special
they would offer to paint people's houses
while they were out at work.

That way when they came home
in the evening they would return
to a freshly painted home!

The business would be called

**THE HICKORY DICKORY DOC
    HOUSE PAINTING COMPANY.**

They would use their garage as an office
and a place to store the paints,
            ladders and paint brushes.

The first task, though, was to divide up
        all the jobs between themselves.

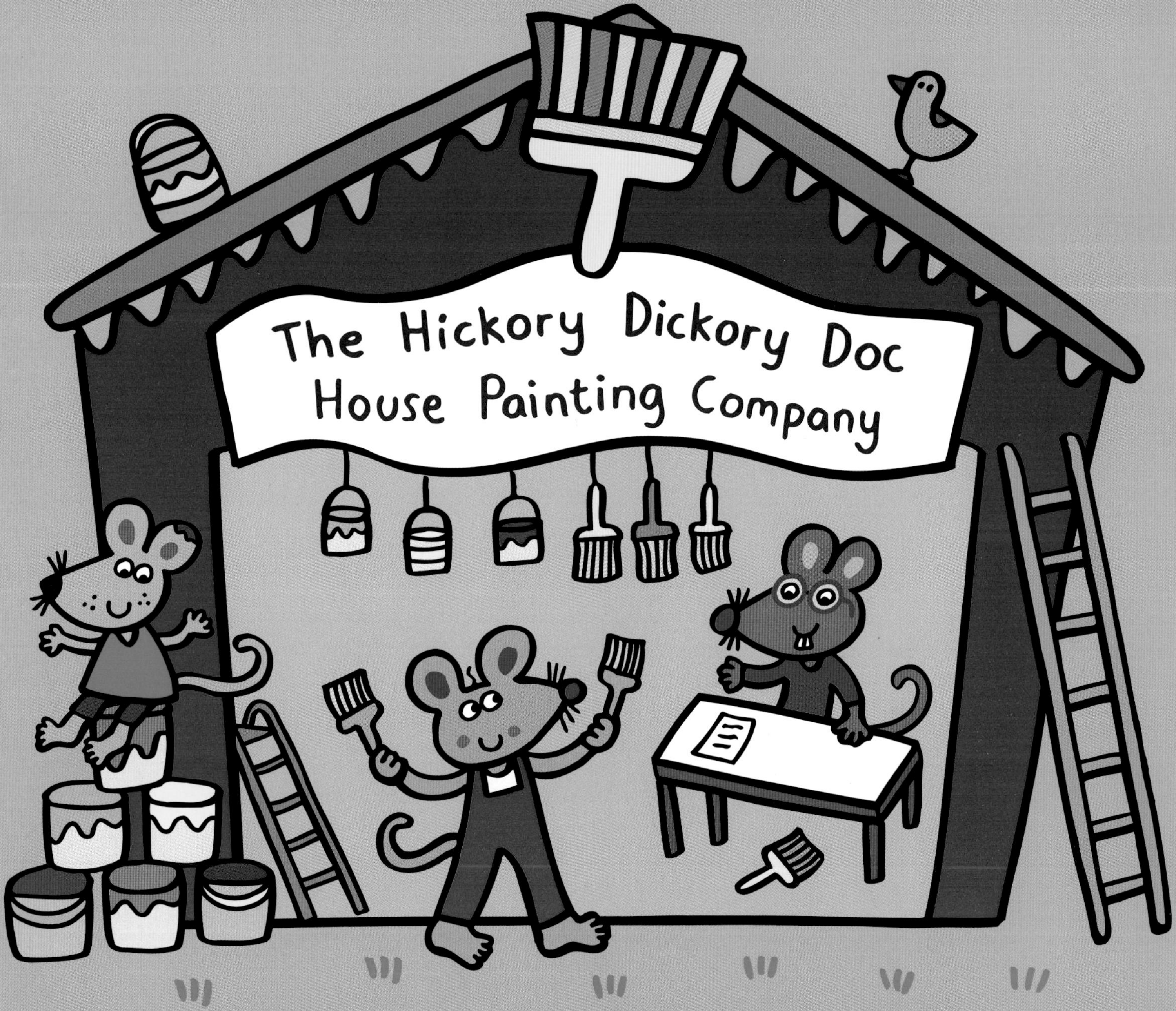
The Hickory Dickory Doc
House Painting Company

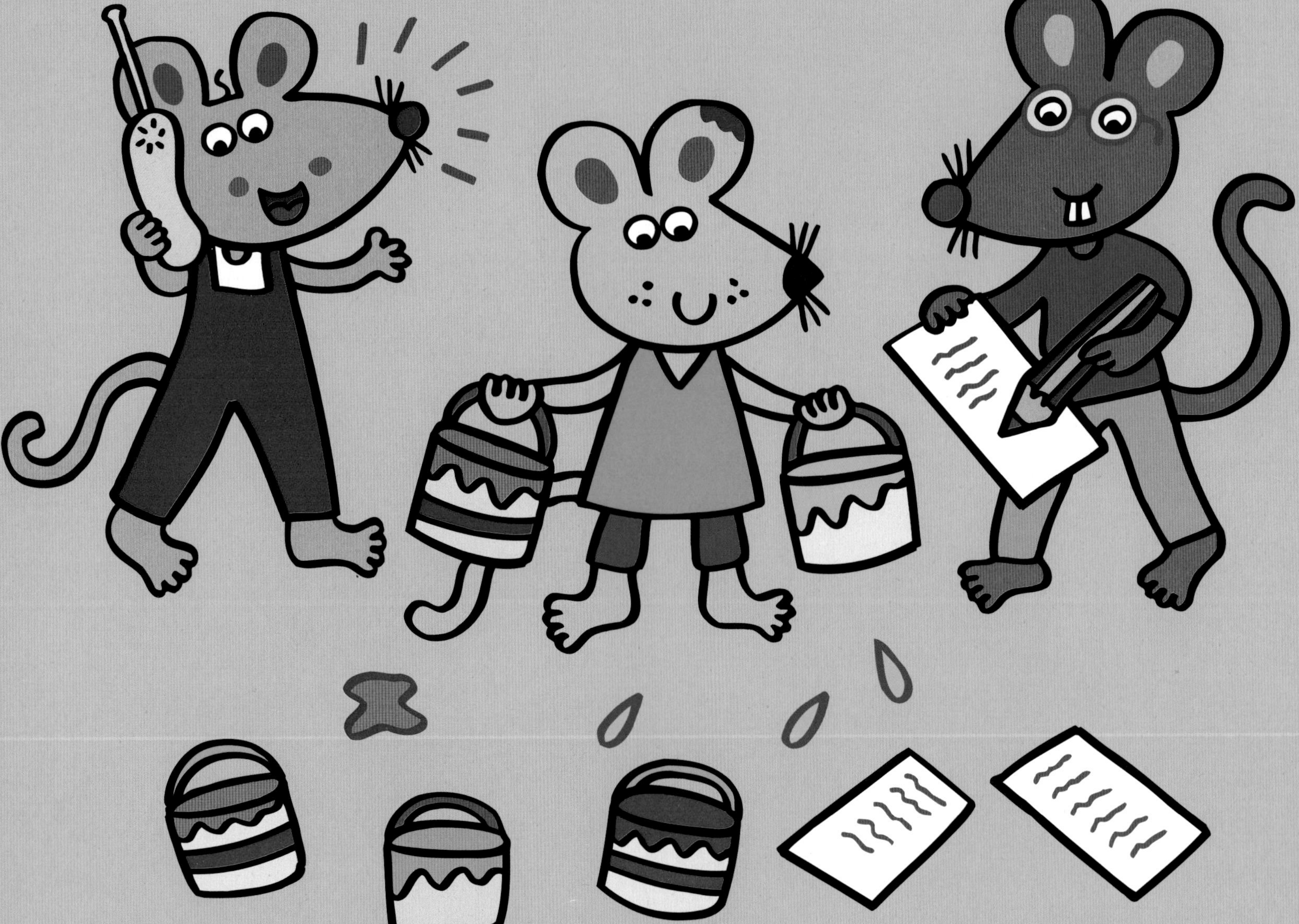

Hickory was a good salesperson. His job was to find customers and offer to have **THE HICKORY DICKORY DOC HOUSE PAINTING COMPANY** paint their homes.

Dickory was the cleverest of the three brothers and he would do the planning. He would make lists of customers, their houses, and their selection of colors.

Doc was the most artistic of the three and he would be able to select and mix any color their customers might want.

Early next morning...

Hickory began by calling on their neighbors, offering to have the brothers paint their homes.

He went to each house, explaining the new business and offering to paint the house in any colors the customer chose.

He told everyone that their house would be completely painted by the time they got home from work.

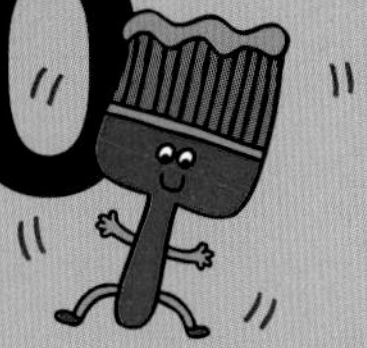

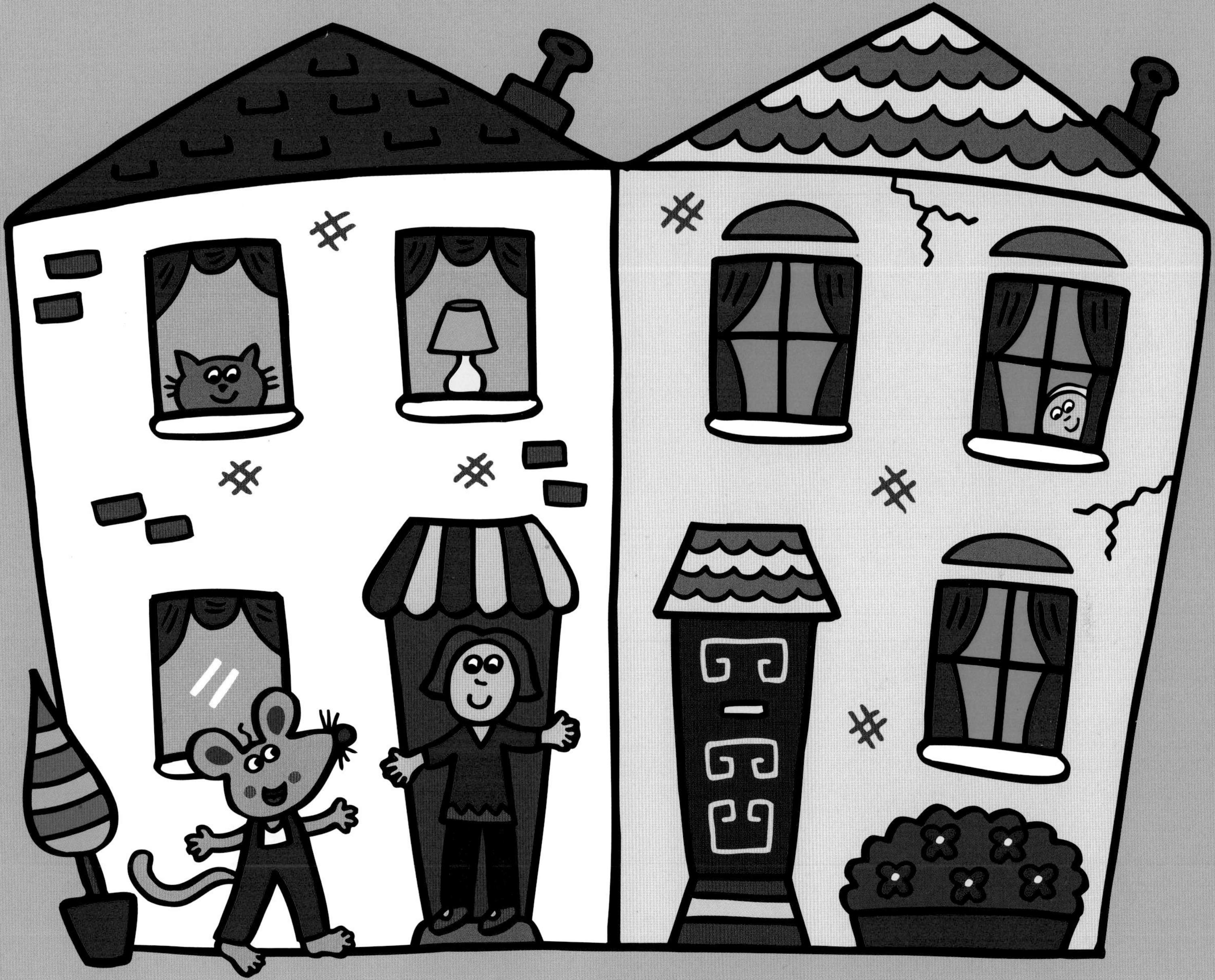

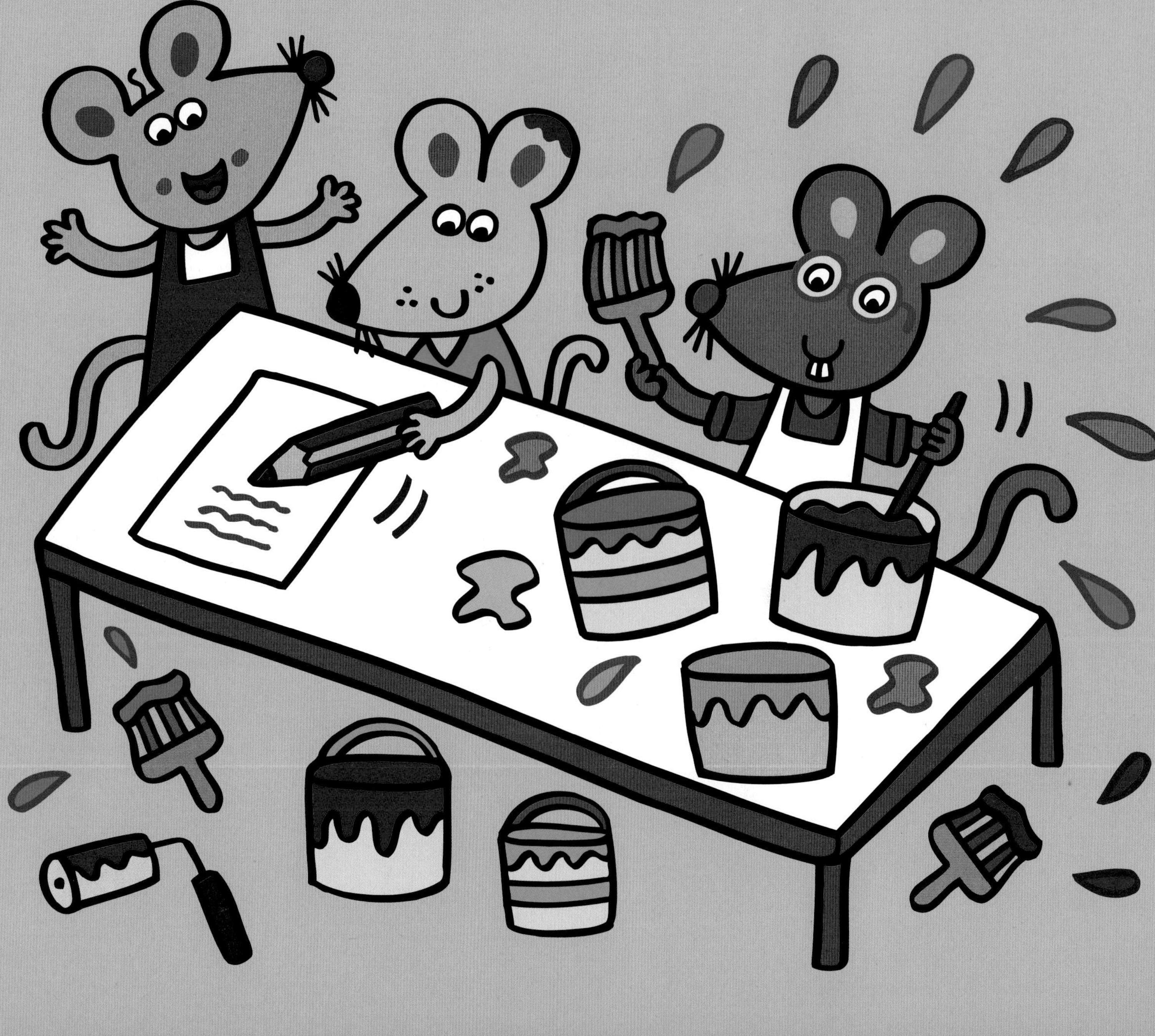

Hickory came back with lots of orders.
Everyone wanted the three brothers
to paint their houses while they were out at work.

Hickory gave the orders from
the customers to **Dickory**.

Dickory wrote them down along
with the colors the customers wanted
and gave the list to **Doc**.

Doc then mixed all the different paints.

Early the next day they would begin
with the first house on the list.

13

So, first thing next morning,
they took their paints,
ladders and paint brushes to
the first house on the list.

All three brothers started working hard
with painting.

14

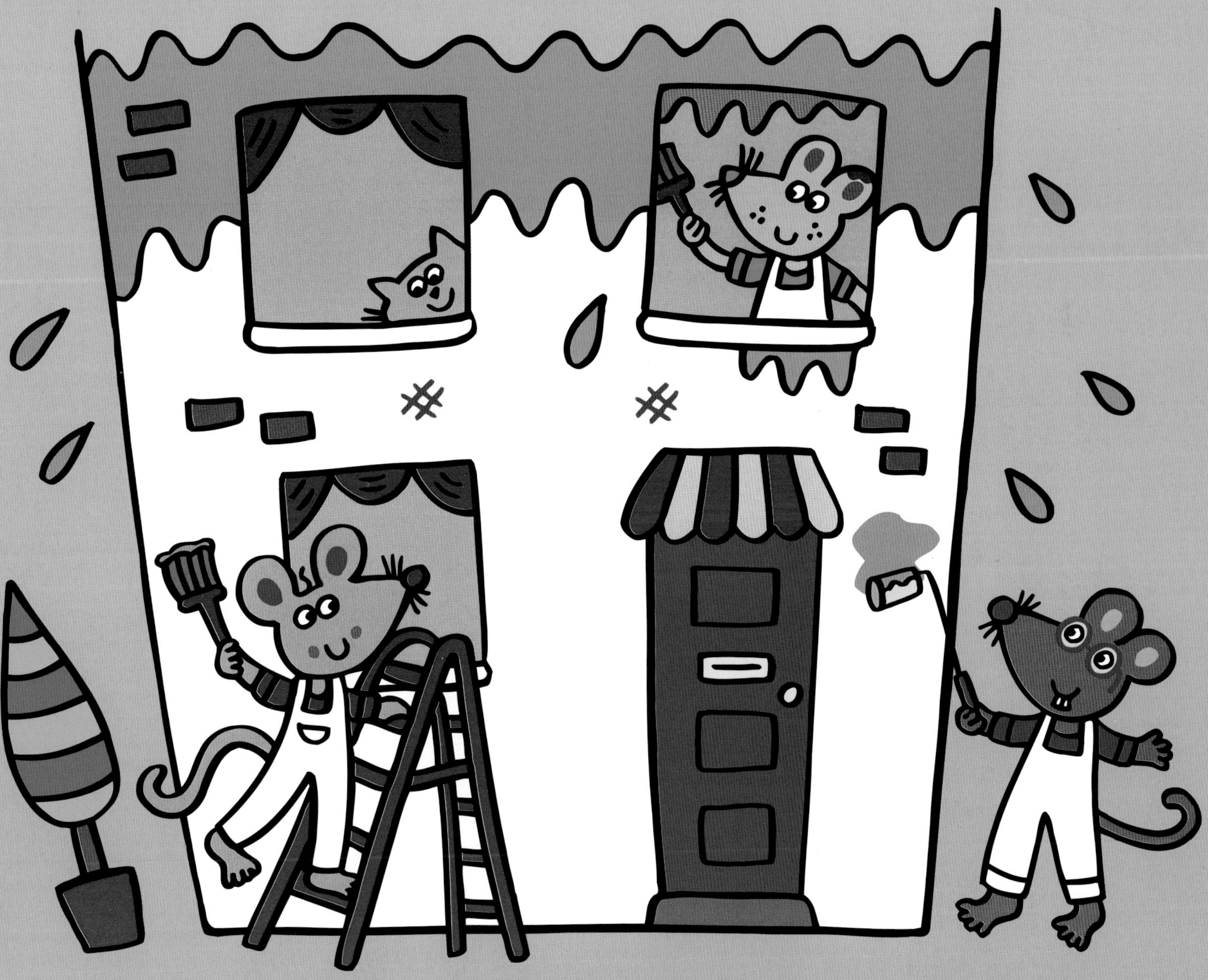

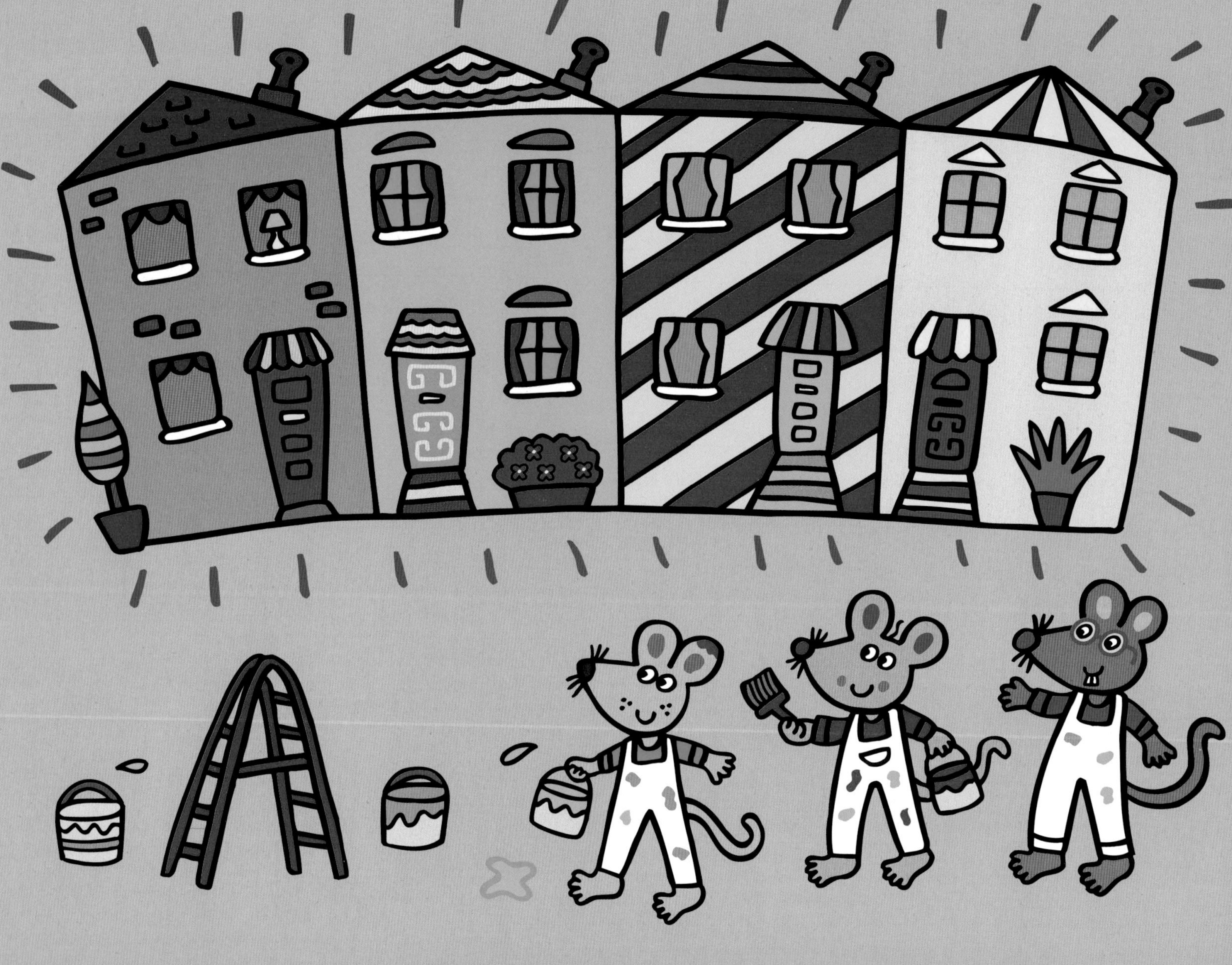

Before they knew it, they had finished
　　not just one but several houses.

They had painted one blue, one green,
　　one green & red, and another yellow & blue.

They carried on working down the street
　　and when they were finished,
　　　　every house was newly painted
　　　　　　in bright, fresh colors.

The three brothers stepped back
　　to admire their work –
　　　　they were very pleased.

Hickory, Dickory and Doc

went home and decided
to celebrate with a big dinner
of crackers and cheese.

They were very tired after their long day's work,
but also very happy.
The day had gone so well,
but it had not gone all right.

Their telephone started to ring.

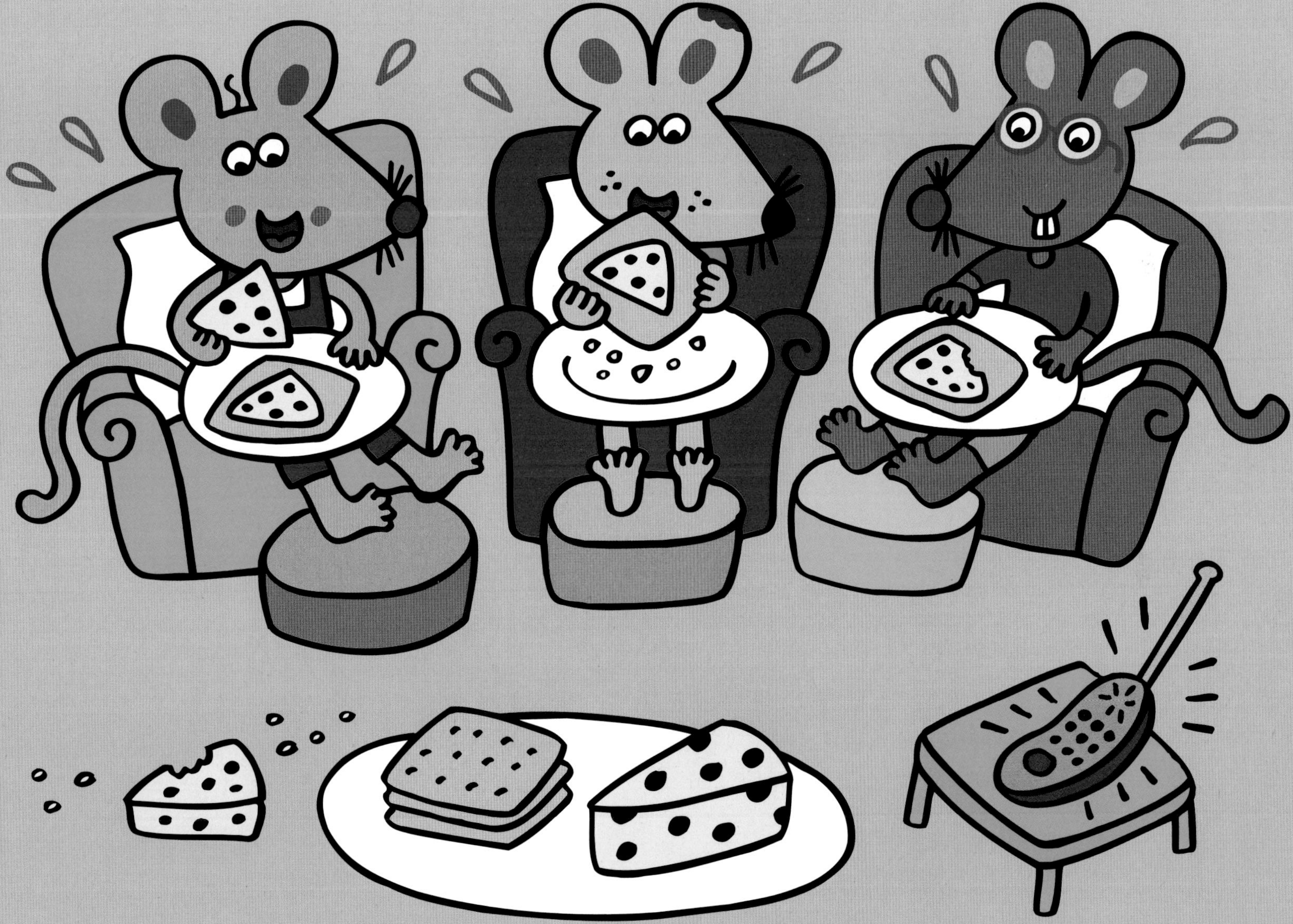

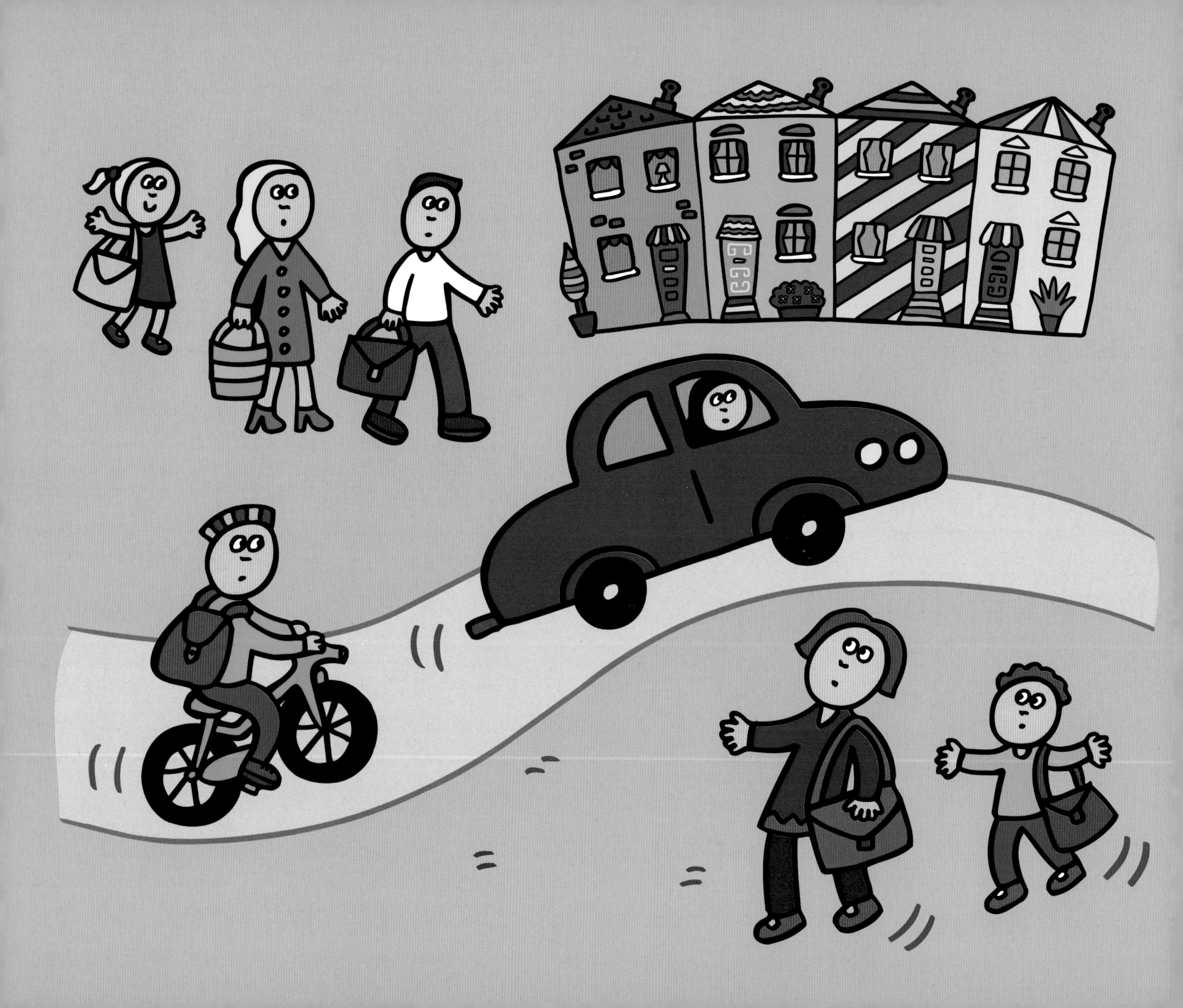

21

It turned out that the houses
were not painted in the colors
they should have been!

People came home from work
and couldn't recognise their own homes
because they weren't the colors
they had chosen!

In fact, some of them
　　　　even went into the wrong houses
because they were so confused
　　　　　by all the wrong colors!

22

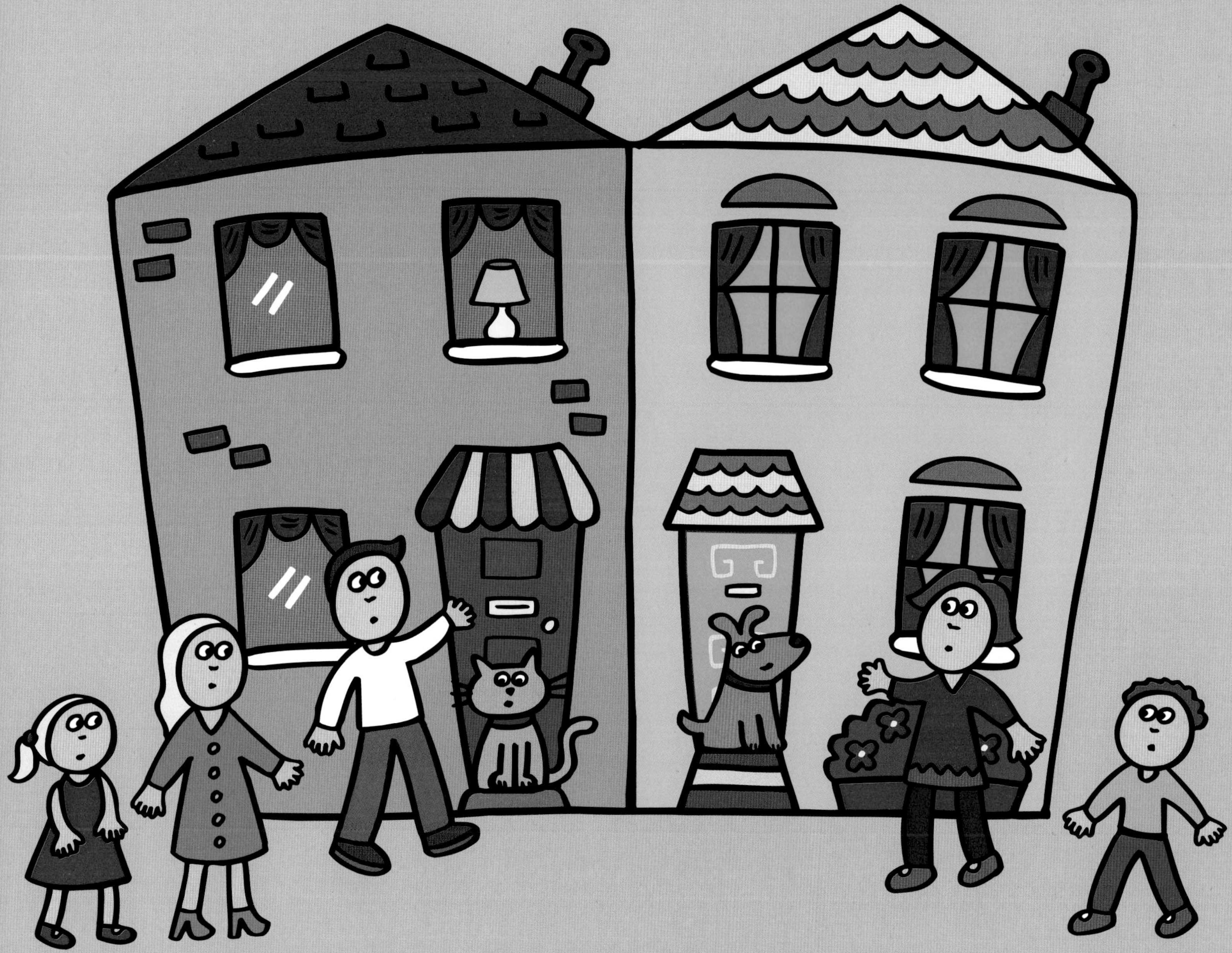

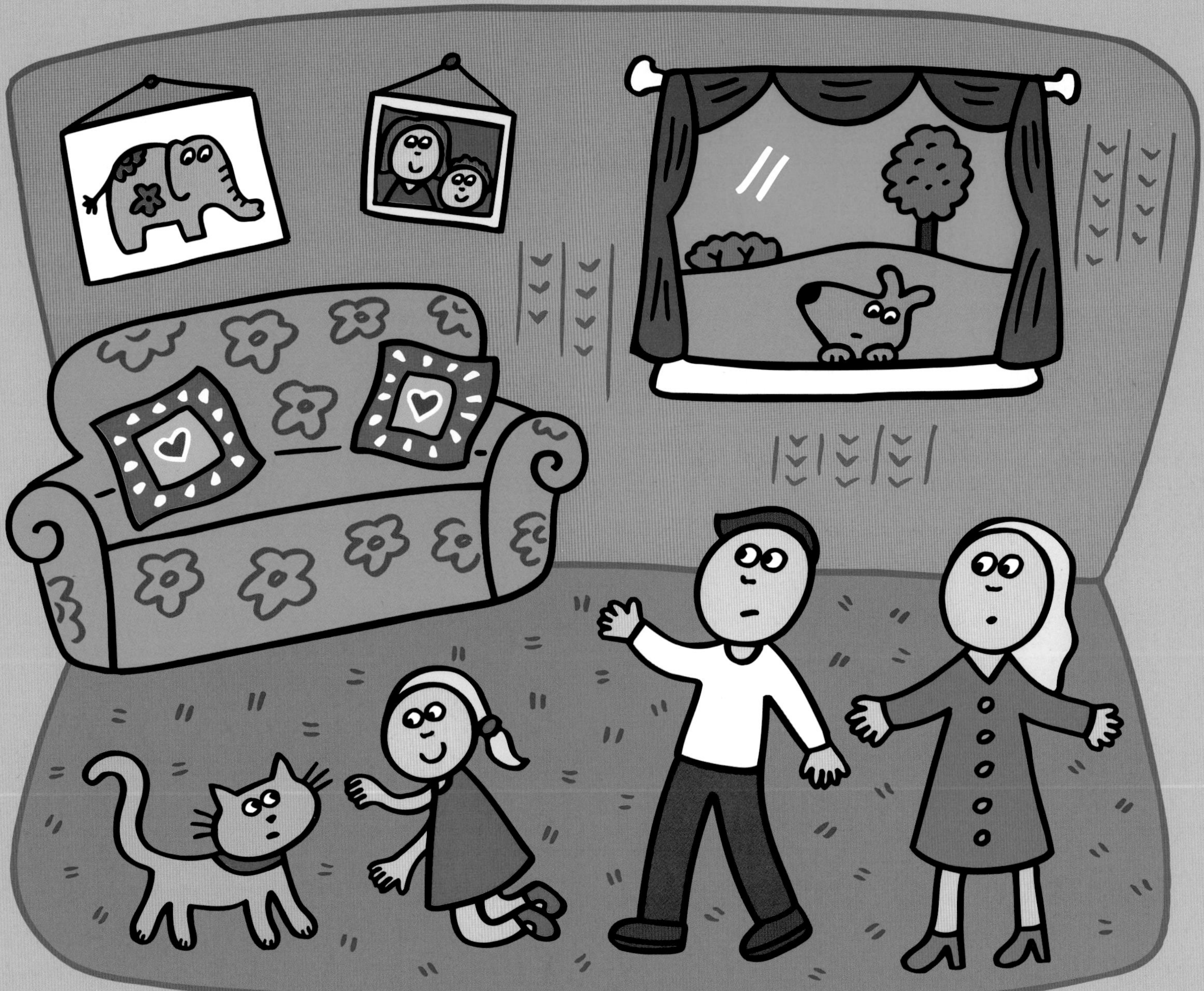

The people who went into the wrong houses
found dogs and cats
that didn't look like theirs.

They also found furniture and pictures
on the walls that were different
from what had been there that morning.

The carpet colors weren't right.

Some even noticed that the cars
in their garages were different
from the ones they owned!

Everyone was confused and upset
to find their favorite things missing.

26

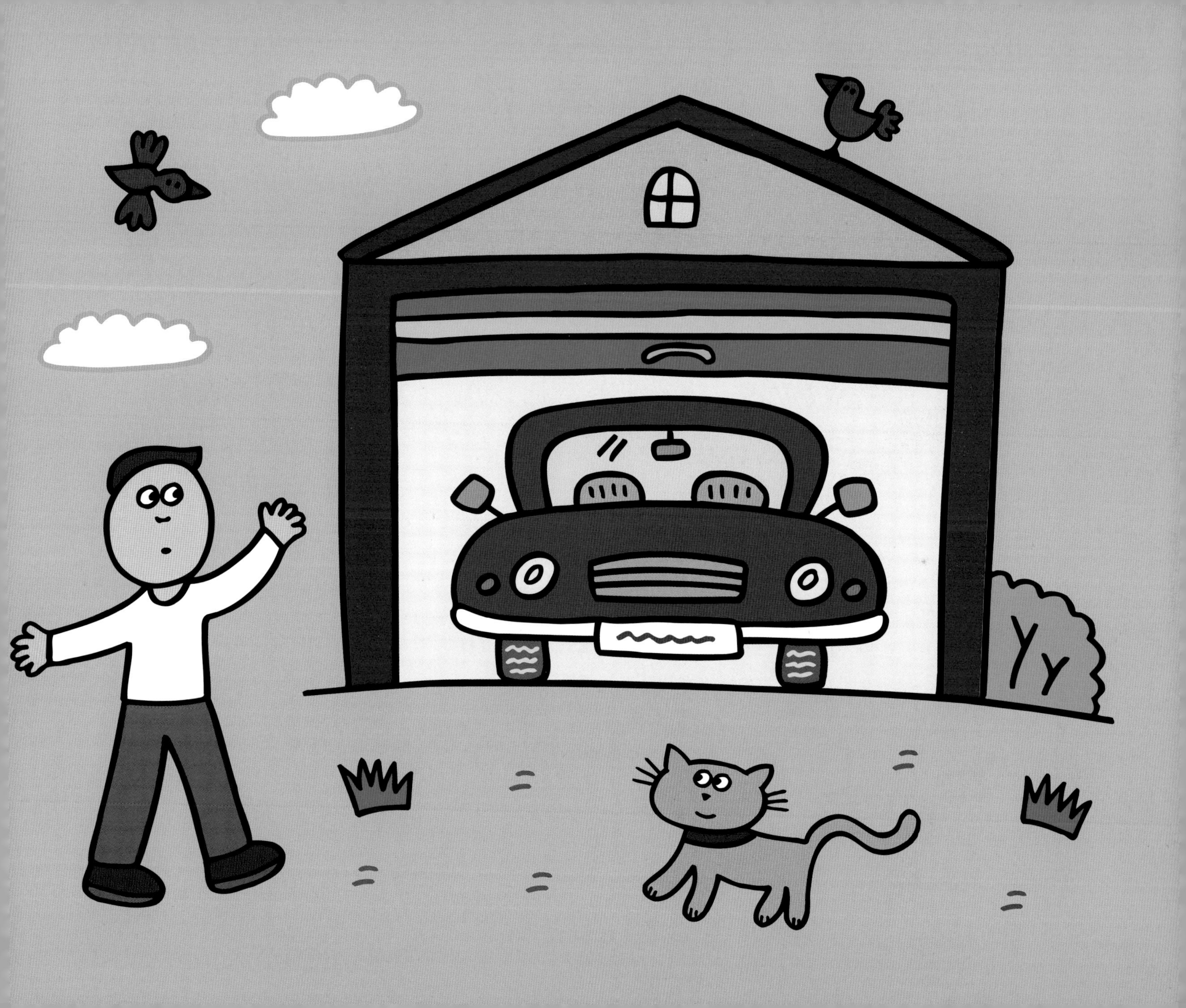

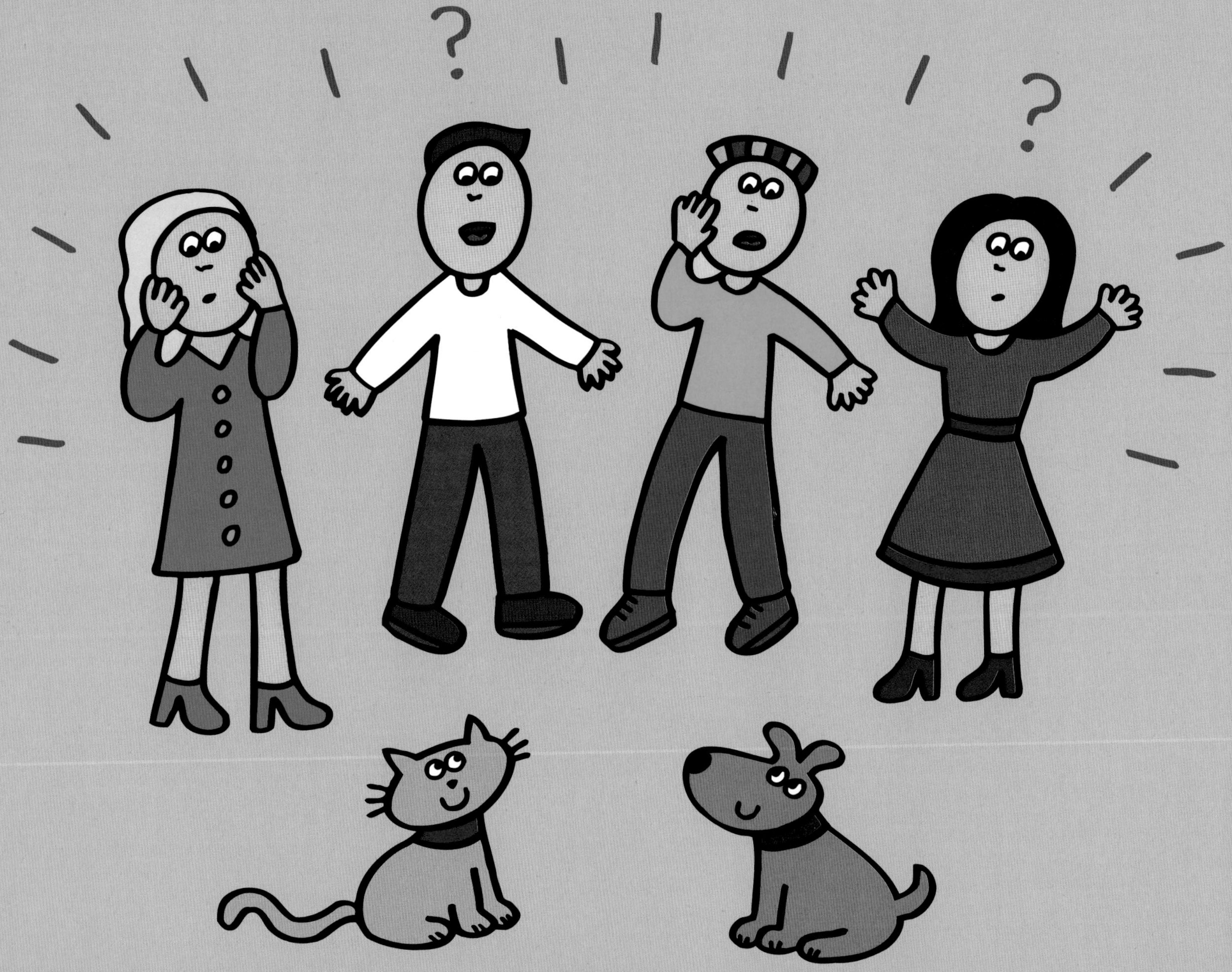

Then they realized: **this isn't my house!**

29

That's when people guessed
what must have happened
and started ringing
the three brothers to complain.

It turned out **Dickory**'s lists of
the customers and their choice of colors
had been turned upside down!

30

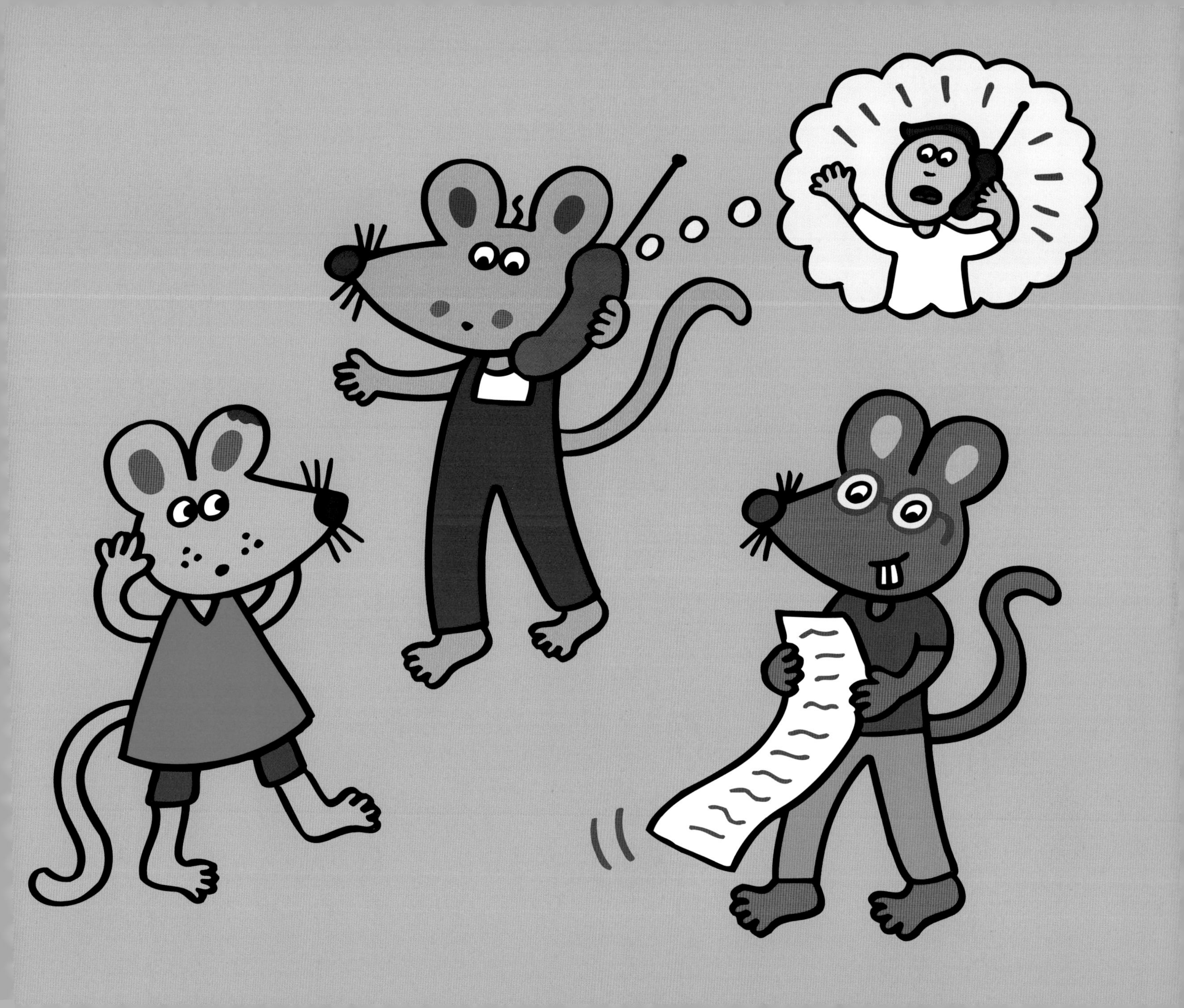

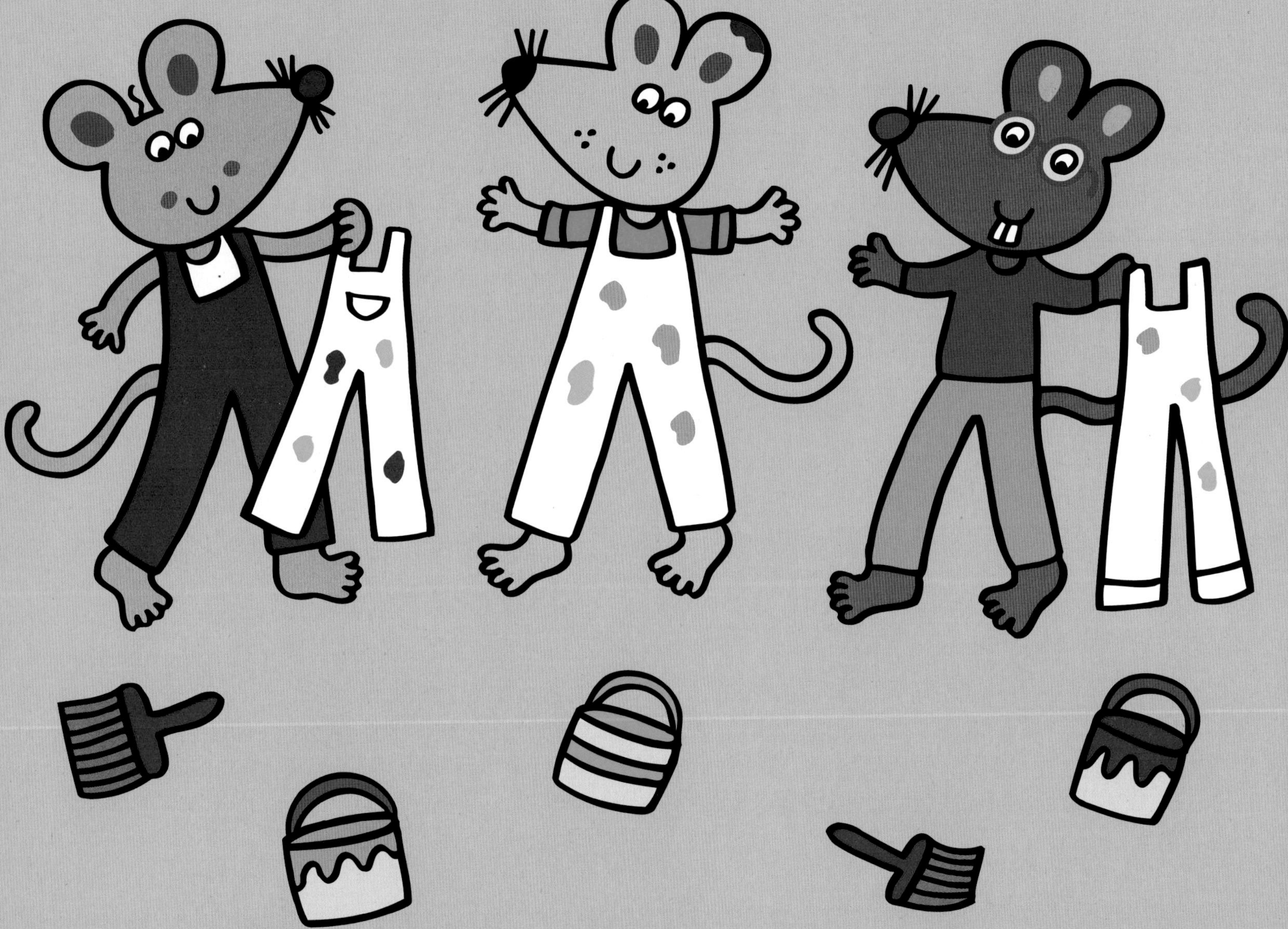

The three brothers had used
the wrong colors on the wrong houses!

They knew they had to do something
quickly to correct their big mistake,
so they put on their overalls and prepared
to repaint the houses in the right colors.

But almost at once one of the neighbors
came running out to stop them!

Even though **Hickory**, **Dickory** and **Doc**
had indeed made a big mistake,
the street looked so colorful and vibrant
that all their customers decided
they wanted to leave
their houses just as they were.

34

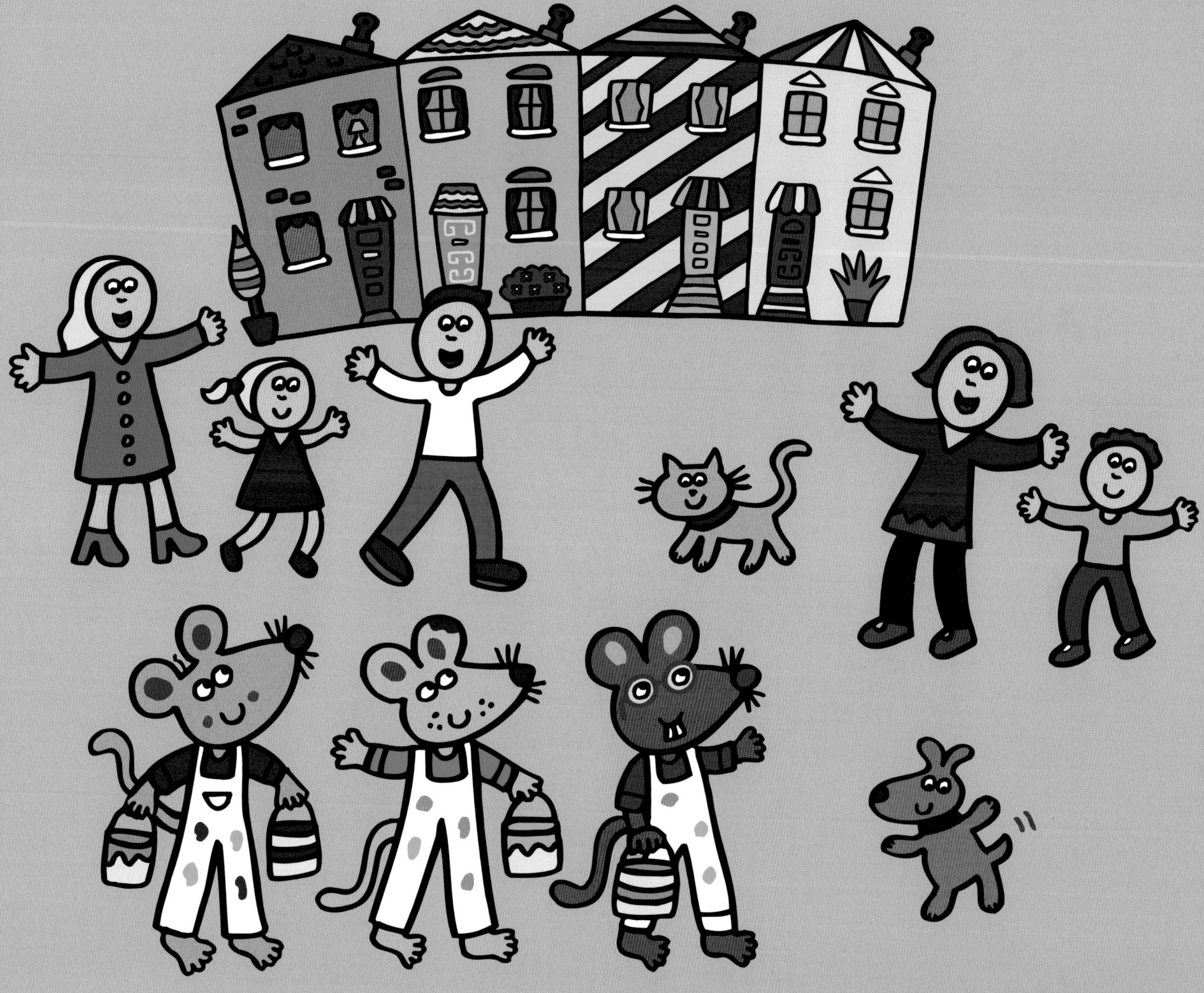

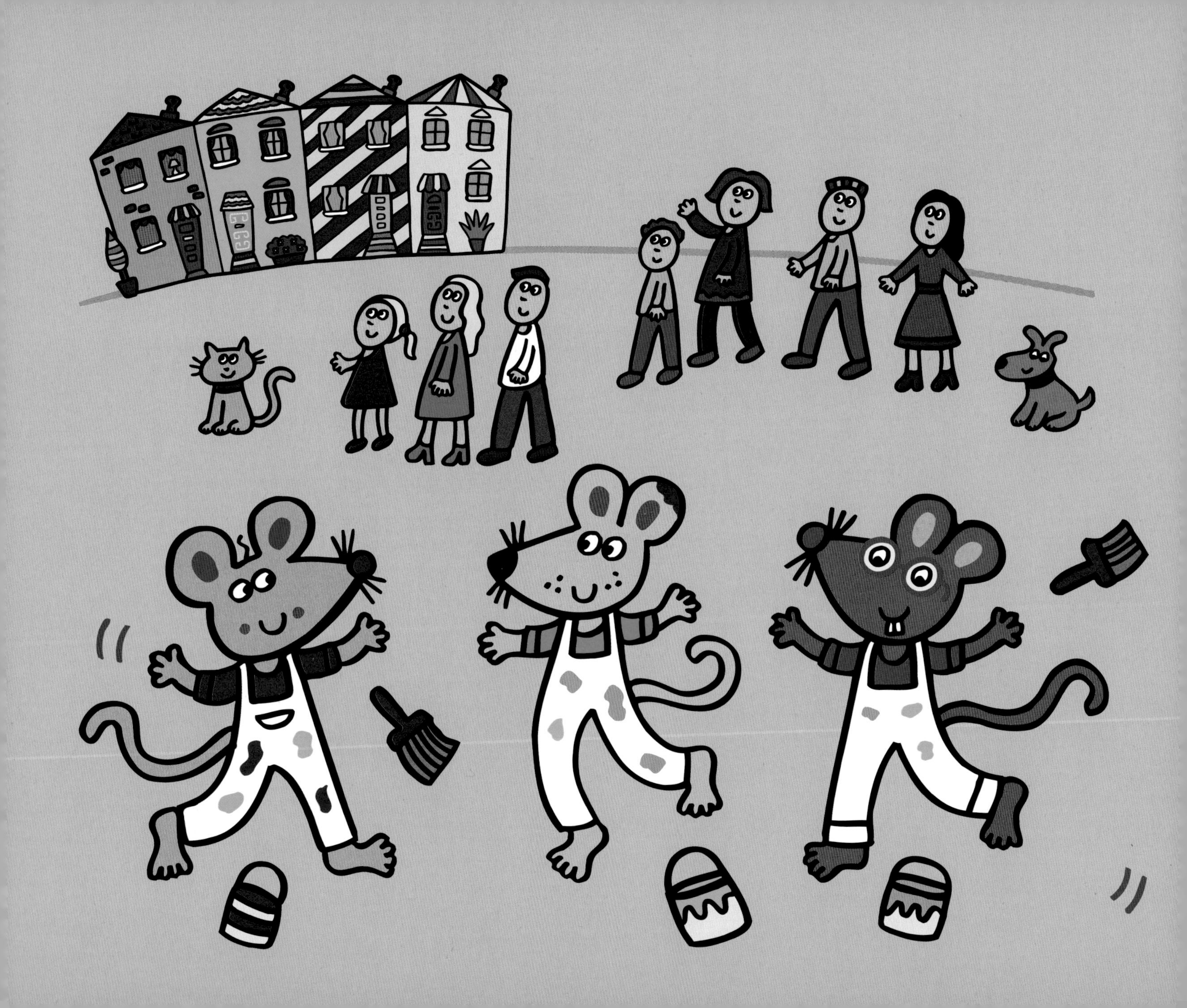

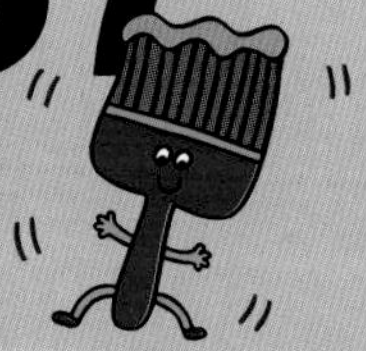

The brothers were so happy
because despite their mistake
they had cheered up the street
with bright colors and all their
customers were outside admiring
the neighborhood's dazzling new look
with smiles on their faces.

So, **Hickory**, **Dickory** and **Doc**'s
first day in their new business
had been a great success after all!

They decided to get a good night's rest.

In the morning, they would start
            painting houses in another street.

But as they got ready for bed,
    Doc turned to his two brothers
            and said that sometimes
                        – just sometimes –
            when you do something wrong,
                        it comes out right.

38

The End

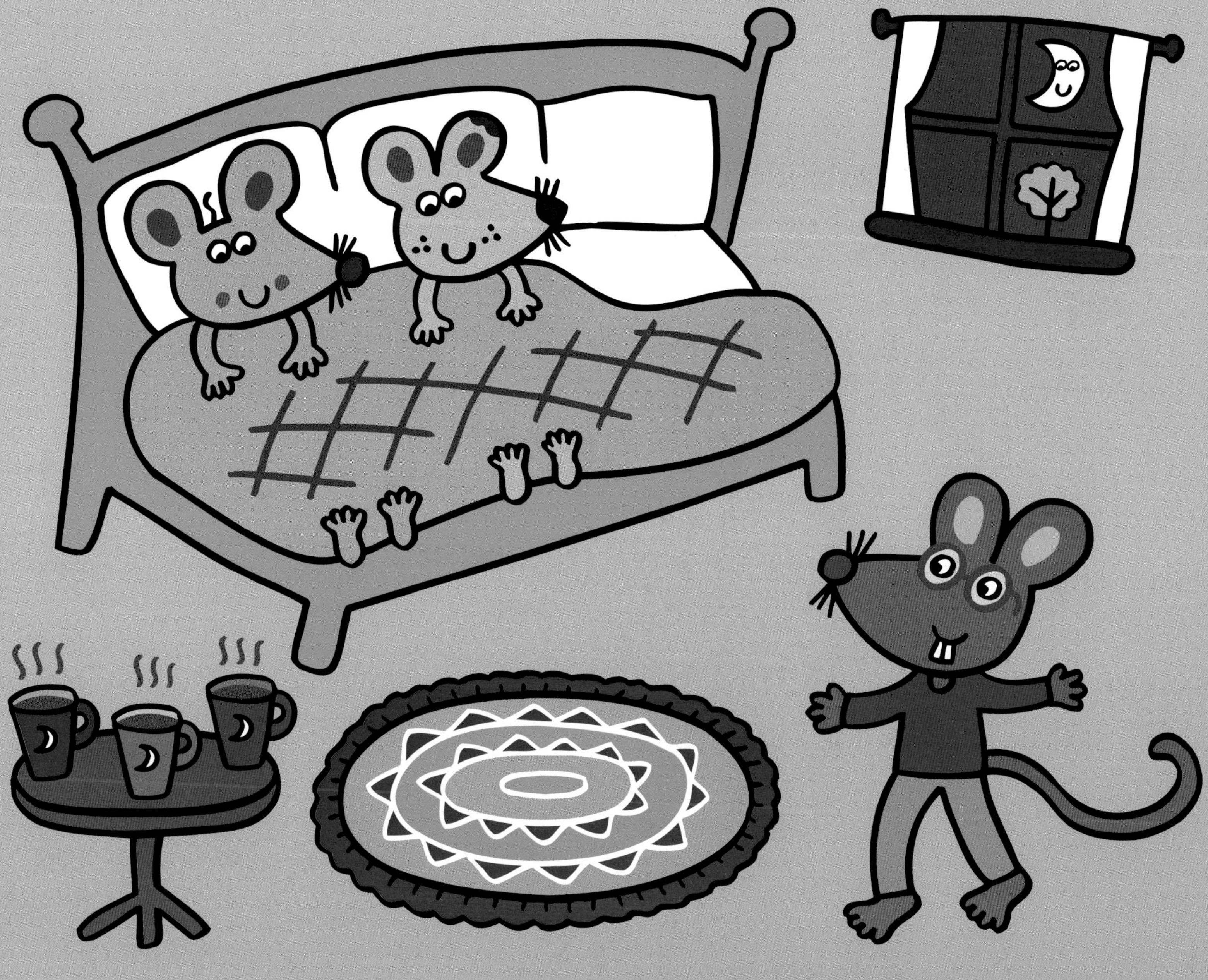

for Mylo and Yasmine

Published by Imagine & Wonder
28 Sycamore Lane, Irvington
New York, NY10533
United States of America.
Telephone: 646.644.0403

Exclusive Distributors: APG

ISBN 978-1-95365-241-6
Library of Congress Control Number:
2021934284

Published by arrangement
between Bish Bash Books and
Imagine & Wonder.

Story by Bob Wise.
Designed and art directed by Michael Bell Design.
Illustrated by Sonia Canals.

Printed in China by
Hung Hing Off-Set Printing Company Limited.

PRINTED WITH
SOY INK
Trademark of American Soybean Association

FSC
www.fsc.org

MIX
Paper from
responsible sources
FSC® C017606

Your guarantee of quality:
As publishers, we strive to produce every book
to the highest commercial standards.
The printing and binding have been planned
to ensure a sturdy, attractive publication
which should give years of enjoyment.
If your copy fails to meet our high standards,
please inform us and we will gladly replace it.

www.imagineandwonder.com

Also available in the lovable mice series...

That Can't Be The Time tells the charming story of three mice brothers who want to start a clock-making business. They are keen and work hard, but after a simple mistake, their first attempt has some rather surprising results!

ISBN 978-1-95365-240-9

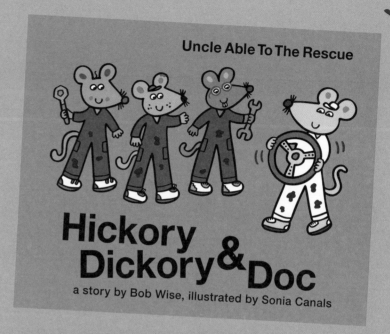

That Can't Be The Time
Hickory Dickory & Doc
a story by Bob Wise, illustrated by Sonia Canals

Uncle Able To The Rescue
Hickory Dickory & Doc
a story by Bob Wise, illustrated by Sonia Canals

Uncle Able To The Rescue is the third story in this popular series featuring three mice who keep starting new businesses. Their car repair shop runs into unforeseen problems that this time they can't solve... until Uncle Able comes to their rescue!

ISBN 978-1-95365-242-3

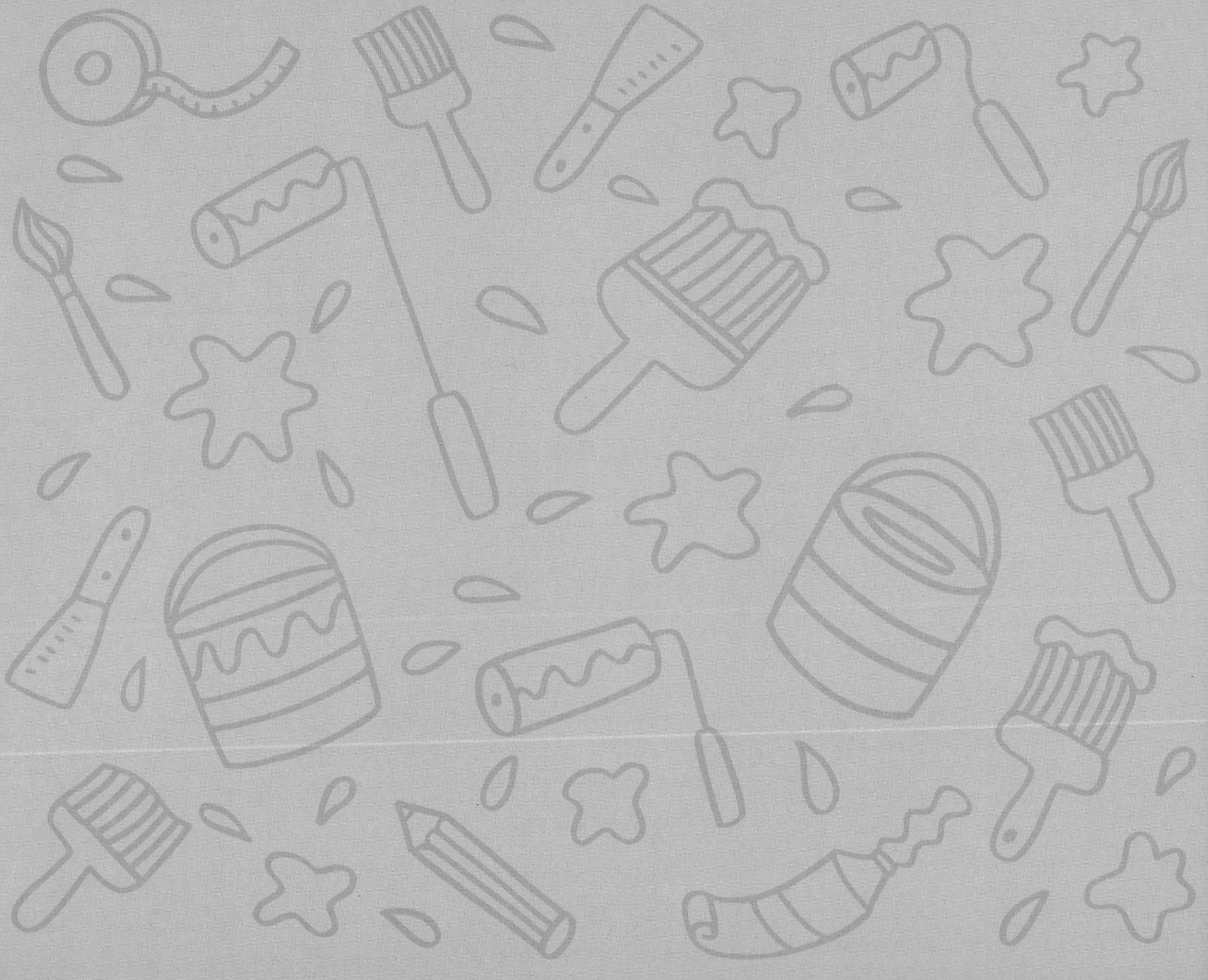